This edition published by Parragon Books Ltd in 2014

Parragon Books Ltd
Chartist House
15–17 Trim Street
Bath BA1 1HA, UK
www.parragon.com

ISBN 978-1-4723-7986-3

Printed in China

Sleeping Beauty

Bath • New York • Cologne • Melbourne • Delhi
Hong Kong • Shenzhen • Singapore • Amsterdam

Long ago, in a far away land, King Stefan and his Queen held a feast to celebrate the birth of their daughter, Aurora. King Hubert and his young son, Phillip, came from a neighbouring kingdom to attend the feast.

The two kings made plans for Phillip and Aurora to marry on the Princess's sixteenth birthday.

Also at the celebrations were the princess's three fairy godmothers, Flora, Fauna and Merryweather. Each of them had a special gift for the Princess.

First, Flora waved her magic wand over the baby's cradle and said, "I give you the gift of beauty."

Then, Fauna waved her wand and said, "I give you the gift of song."

Finally, Merryweather fluttered over to the cradle. She raised her wand to grant the third gift, when...

Suddenly, there was a crack of lightning. Maleficent, the wicked fairy stormed in. She was furious that she had not been invited to the celebrations.

Stroking her pet raven, Maleficent glared at the baby Princess. "I also have a gift for you," she hissed. "Before the sun sets on your sixteenth birthday, you will prick your finger on the spindle of a spinning wheel and die!"

Maleficent threw back her head and laughed wickedly. Then, she disappeared in a cloud of purple smoke.

Merryweather gave
a gentle cough. "I still have
my gift for the Princess,"
she reminded the horrified
King and Queen.

She went over to the cradle
and whispered, "When the spindle
pricks your finger, you will not die.
Instead, you will fall into a deep,
enchanted sleep. From this slumber
you shall wake when true love's
kiss the spell shall break."

The King
was still terribly
worried about his
daughter's safety.
He ordered every
spinning wheel
in the kingdom to be burned. Then, he and
the Queen sadly agreed to the fairy godmothers' plan. They
took Aurora far away to a place where Maleficent wouldn't
be able to find her until her sixteenth birthday had passed.

Flora, Fauna and Merryweather renamed the Princess Briar Rose. They moved into a little cottage in the woods. There, the fairies put away their magic wands and disguised themselves as simple peasant women.

As the years passed, Maleficent kept searching for the Princess, but she never found her.

As the Princess's sixteenth birthday drew nearer, Maleficent sent her trusted pet raven to try and find her. It was Maleficent's last chance.

The morning
of Briar Rose's
birthday finally
arrived. The three
fairies sent her to
collect berries in
the woods, while
they prepared some
birthday surprises.
After gathering the berries,
Briar Rose rested in a woodland glade.
She sang about falling in love with a
handsome prince.

Her woodland
friends found a cloak,
a hat and a pair of
boots that had been
left in the forest. They
dressed up as a make-believe
prince. Briar
Rose joined
in their
game, dancing
and singing with them.

The clothes belonged to Prince Phillip, who, after a long ride, was resting in the woods with his horse. Phillip was enchanted by the beautiful singing coming through the trees and went to see who it was. The moment they met, Briar Rose and the handsome stranger fell in love. They felt sure that they had met somewhere before. When it was time for Briar Rose to leave, they arranged to meet that evening at the cottage in the woods.

Meanwhile, the three fairies set about making their birthday surprises. But before long they were in a terrible muddle! Fauna had baked a birthday cake. But the mixture was too runny and the cake was lopsided!

Flora and Merryweather had made a special gown for Briar Rose, but it was an awfully funny shape!

"It's no use," said Merryweather. "We need to use magic to sort this out. I'll fetch the wands."

Before
they dared to
use their wands,
the fairies blocked up
every gap in the cottage.
They had to stop any magic
dust from escaping and alerting
Maleficent to their hideaway. But
they forgot to block the chimney!

It was so wonderful to be able
to use magic again! Flora waved
her wand and a beautiful pink
gown appeared.

Then Merryweather waved her
wand and changed the gown to blue.
Flora changed it back to pink. All the time,
magic dust was escaping from the chimney.

Maleficent's raven was searching nearby. He saw
the magic dust and decided to fly down and investigate.

When Briar Rose returned to the cottage
she thanked her fairy godmothers for the
beautiful new gown and the delicious cake.

"This is the
happiest day of
my life," she said.
Then she told
them about the handsome
stranger she had met in the
woods. He planned to visit her
at the cottage that very evening.

"It's time we told Briar Rose
the truth," said Fauna.

So, Briar Rose learnt that she was really a princess and would soon have to marry Prince Phillip. "Today you must return to the palace and start your new life," said Flora. Up on the chimney, Maleficent's raven smiled.

Briar Rose was heartbroken. She didn't want to marry a prince. She had fallen in love with the handsome stranger she had met in the woods.

By now, the raven had heard enough. He flew off to tell his mistress that the search for Princess Aurora was over.

As soon as darkness fell, the fairy godmothers led Briar Rose through the forest to the palace.

They had no idea that Maleficent was already there, lying in wait for them.

At the palace, the fairy godmothers left Aurora in a quiet room to rest. Suddenly, a strange glowing light appeared. Aurora followed it in a trance. It led her up a winding staircase to an attic room.

Inside the room Maleficent
was waiting by a spinning wheel.
Aurora had never seen a spinning
wheel before. The wicked fairy
urged the princess to touch it.
Aurora reached out and pricked
her finger on the spindle. In an
instant she had fallen into a deep sleep.

Before long, the fairy godmothers found Aurora lying
by the spinning wheel. They quickly cast a sleeping spell
over the entire palace.

Luckily, the fairies had discovered that Prince Phillip
was the stranger with whom Briar Rose had fallen in love.
Only his kiss could wake her! So, while everyone was
asleep, the fairies thought of a plan. They would return to
the cottage, find Phillip and bring him back to the palace.

But they were too late! Maleficent and her soldiers had already found the Prince waiting at the cottage and captured him.

Maleficent took Phillip back to her castle where she threw him into her deepest, darkest dungeon. She fastened him to the wall with chains and left him there to die.

When the
fairies couldn't find
Prince Phillip at the
cottage, they soon realized Maleficent must have
captured him. They quickly made their way to her castle.

As soon as it was safe, the fairies magically appeared
in the dungeon and freed the prince. They waved their
wands and armed him with a magic shield of virtue and
a gleaming sword of truth.

Then, the Prince jumped on his horse and galloped
off to King Stefan's palace to rescue Princess Aurora.

When Maleficent
discovered that the Prince
had escaped she roared with rage.
She cast a spell that surrounded the palace
with a forest of thorns. But Phillip was able to cut
his way through with
his magic sword.

Suddenly, a huge
and terrible black
dragon appeared.
The dragon laughed
wickedly – it was Maleficent! Prince Phillip
held up his magic shield so that the scorching flames could
not harm him.

The battle had begun! The dragon soared into the
air and swooped down towards Prince Phillip. The Prince
hurled his magic sword at the dragon's chest. The beast
crashed to the ground. Maleficent was dead!

Prince Phillip raced towards the palace. He quickly found the room where Sleeping Beauty lay. As he gently kissed her, she opened her eyes – the spell was broken!

The fairy godmothers' spell was broken too. All round the palace, people began to wake from their enchanted sleep.

The King and Queen were
delighted to have their
beloved daughter back
again. That evening,
a magnificent ball
was held to celebrate
the wedding of Phillip
and Aurora. The Princess
was dressed in the beautiful
blue gown, but Flora couldn't resist

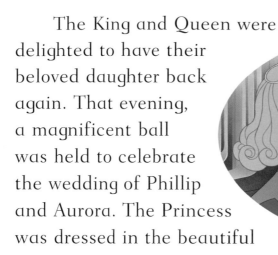

turning the blue gown back to pink.
Then Merryweather turned
it back to blue and so it
went on, pink…
blue…pink…

The Princess danced
happily in the arms
of her Prince, while
their proud fathers
looked on.
A dream come
true, the Prince
and Princess lived
happily ever after.